For da Papa and da Baby.
My favorite love story.

SM

For my favorite furry friend and
my family: the best playmates.

KK

First edition 2021

Library of Congress Catalog Card Number pending
ISBN 978-1-5362-0840-5

21 22 23 24 25 26 CCP 10 9 8 7 6 5 4 3 2 1

Printed in Shenzhen, Guangdong, China

This book was typeset in Garden Essential and hand-lettered.
The illustrations were created digitally.

Candlewick Press
99 Dover Street
Somerville, Massachusetts 02144

www.candlewick.com

Atticus Caticus

Sarah Maizes   illustrated by Kara Kramer

CANDLEWICK PRESS

Atticus. Cat-ticus. Rat-a-tat-tat-ticus.

Time to wake up, sleepy cat-ticus, Atticus.

He blinks
and he winks
as he lifts
from my bed.

He streeeeeeeeeeeetches,

he huuuuuuunches,

yawns with his whole head.

Atticus Caticus jumps . . .

SPLAT-
a-tat-taticus!

Shake, shake, shake, shake.
He can hear breakfast call.

He bolts from my room and
he shoots down the hall.

Atticus Caticus,
ears like a
bat-tat-ticus!

He gobbles his food
without any delay,
then drinks from my glass
while I'm looking away.

Atticus Caticus, tummy so fat-ticus!

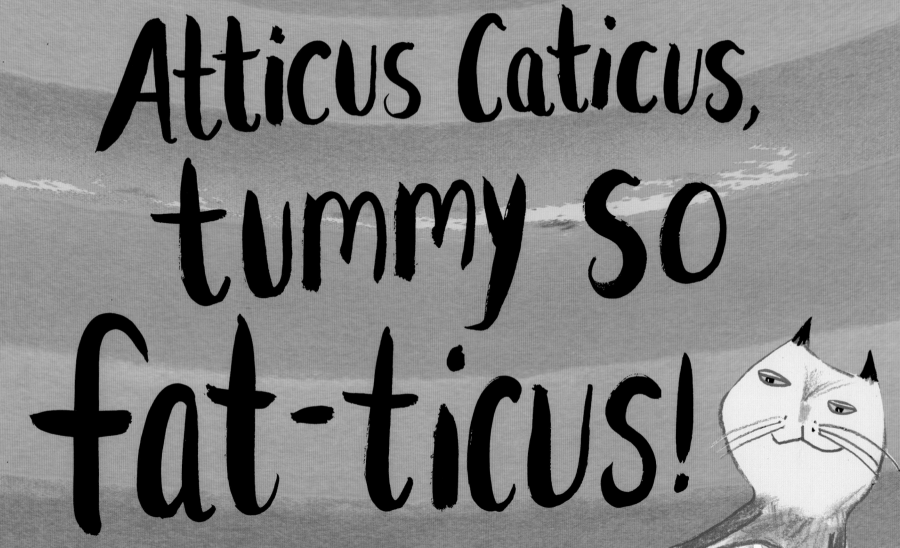

Bowl empty, he searches for sun on the floor.
Then he lies there . . . and lies there . . .

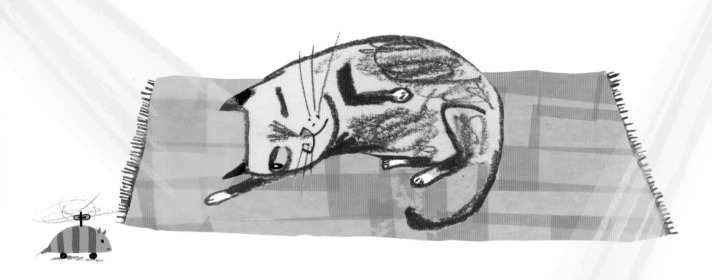

and lies there some more.

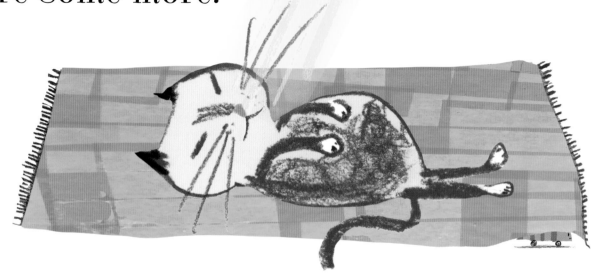

Atticus Caticus,
flat-a-tat-tat-ticus.

A belly so tempting.
He sees me come close.
His whiskers spread wide.
He twitches his nose.

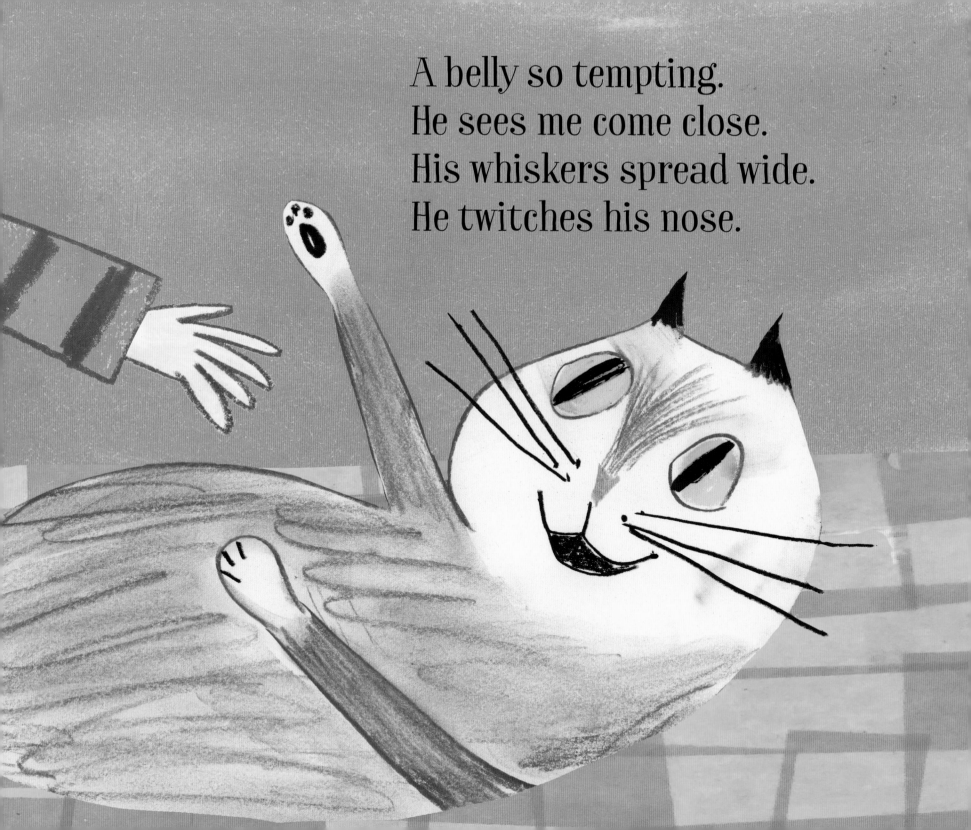

Atticus Caticus, why must you SCAT-tat-ticus?

He darts to the sill as a bird comes to eat.

She chirps and he chitters. He's hoping they'll meet.

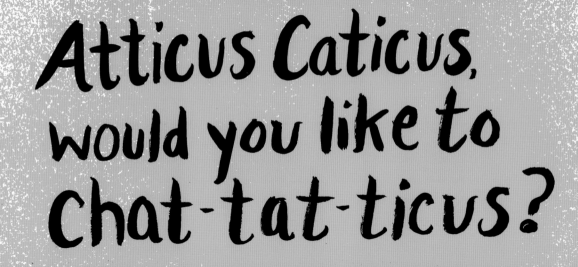

Atticus Caticus,
would you like to
chat-tat-ticus?

I dangle some string as he jumps in the air,

then he sharpens his nails on my mom's favorite chair.

Atticus Caticus,
Scrit-
scrit-
scrat,
Scrat-
ticus.

The afternoon passes
with treats and a nap.
I'd get one myself
if he weren't on my lap!

Atticus Caticus,
snack
attack-atticus.

I head to the bathroom.
He creeps down the hall.
He waits for my toes
as he lurks by the wall.

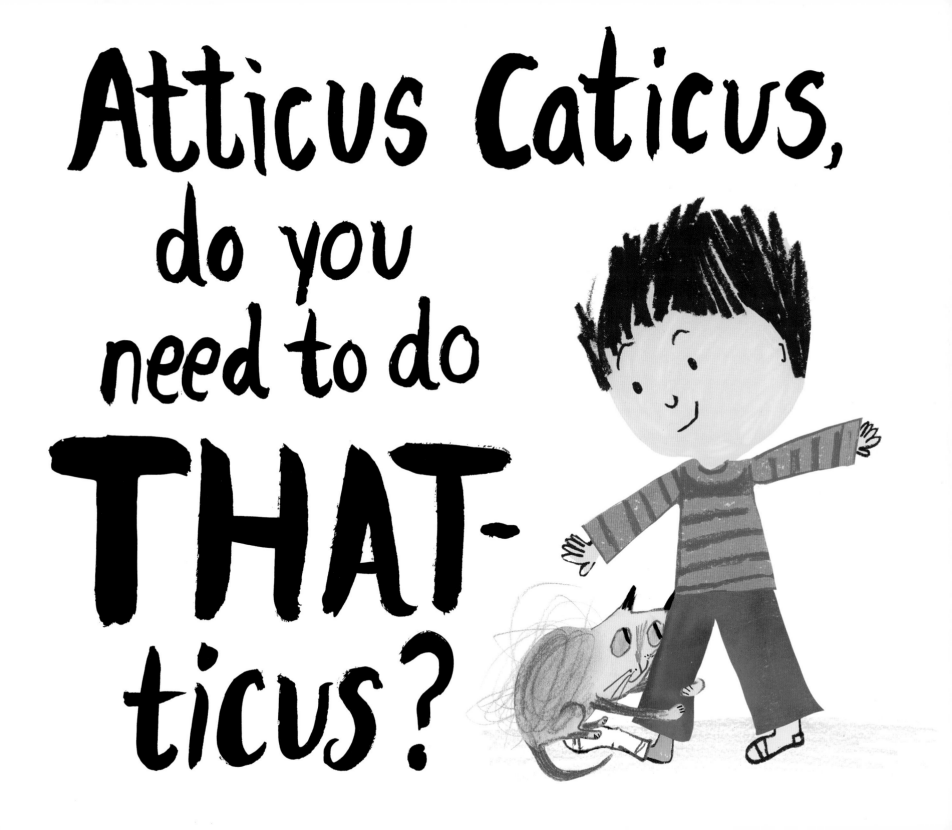

Atticus Caticus, do you need to do THAT-ticus?

I get in the tub and
he comes to get clean.
He licks and he licks—
he's a licking machine.

Atticus Caticus
bathes on a bath mat-ticus.

It's time for lights-out, so he jumps on my bed.

Knead,

knead,

plunk, purrrrrrr . . . and he sleeps on my head.

Atticus Caticus
is a hat-
a-tat-taticus.

Good night, Atticus.
You are one cool cat-tat-ticus.

...Pat-Pat-Pat-Pat-ticus.